Monoliths
Giants of Stone

Heather Hammonds

Contents

Aboriginal and Torres Strait Islander peoples are advised that this text may contain images of people who have passed away.

Monoliths: Giants of Stone

What Are Monoliths?

Monoliths are enormous rocks or stones that rise high above the areas around them.
These giants of stone are often hundreds of metres tall, and can be seen from a long way away.

Monoliths are found in many parts of the world, from hot deserts to the frozen seas of **Antarctica**.

Zuma Rock is a monolith in Nigeria, a country in Africa.

Monoliths can have different and interesting shapes.
These are often caused by **erosion**.

Some monoliths have rounded shapes,
while others have tall, pointed **peaks** or very steep rock walls.

There are monoliths with snow and ice on them, too.

Devils Tower National Monument is a monolith in Wyoming, USA.

People have been amazed by monoliths for thousands of years.

Some monoliths are very important to the communities of **First Nations peoples** that live around them. They are **sacred** places to these peoples.

Uluru is a monolith that is sacred to the Anangu people of the Northern Territitory, Australia.

Today, monoliths attract many tourists.
People travel long distances to take photos of the monoliths and learn about them.

Rock climbers enjoy the challenge of climbing to the top of some of the tallest monoliths.

Other monoliths are easier to climb, and people can hike to the top of them.

People can climb a long staircase to get to the top of the Rock of Guatape in Colombia, a country in South America.

Uluru

Location: Uluru-Kata Tjuta National Park, Northern Territory, Australia

Uluru is found in the central part of Australia and rises 348 metres above the flat desert.

Uluru is the tip of a gigantic rock that formed millions of years ago.
The rest of the rock is buried several kilometres underground.

The Anangu (say: *Arn-an-oo*) people are the **traditional owners** of Uluru. They have lived on the land around Uluru for thousands of years.

Uluru's rounded shape has been caused by erosion over millions of years.

Many visitors travel to Uluru every year. They can walk around the base of the rock and learn about it from the Anangu people.

Visitors to Uluru cannot climb the rock, as it is sacred to the Anangu people.

A traditional Anangu owner guides visitors at Uluru.

El Capitan

Location: Yosemite National Park, California, USA

The huge monolith El Capitan
is found in Yosemite (say: *Yo-sem-i-tee*) National Park.
It is very high, at 2307 metres tall.
El Capitan and the land around it were formed by **glaciers**
flowing around the monolith over millions of years.

Rock climbers travel to El Capitan to climb its steep rock walls.
Some of its hardest climbs can take several days to complete.

Tourists can go hiking on and around El Capitan.

Horsetail Fall is a waterfall that runs down one side of El Capitan in winter and spring.
Each year, during the second half of February,
people come to watch the waterfall at sunset.
The sun turns it a fiery red colour!

Horsetail Fall on the side of El Capitan glows orange and red at sunset.

The Rock of Gibraltar

Location: Gibraltar, South-west Europe

The Rock of Gibraltar is found in the small British **territory** of Gibraltar. It is 426 metres high and is a well-known tourist attraction. Its steep, pale grey cliffs form a triangle shape that is often photographed.

Visitors can hike or take a cable car to the top of the rock.

The Rock of Gibraltar towers over tall buildings by the sea.

A **nature reserve** on the Rock of Gibraltar is home to many plants and animals.
The animals there include some monkeys called Barbary macaques (say: *ma-carks*).
The Barbary macaques are the only wild monkeys in Europe.

A Barbary macaque rests in the sun at the Rock of Gibraltar's nature reserve.

Many tunnels have been dug into the Rock of Gibraltar.
Tourists can visit these tunnels.

Bukit Kelam

Location: Bukit Kelam Nature Park, West Kalimantan, Indonesia

A monolith known as Bukit Kelam
rises up out of tropical rainforest in Indonesia.
This huge, dome-shaped granite rock
is around 1000 metres high.
Clouds hang low over its top during wet weather.
Many rainforest plants grow on its steep, rocky sides.
Bukit Kelam is the largest rock in Indonesia.

Visitors can hike through the rainforest around Bukit Kelam. They can also climb to the top of the huge rock on metal ladders.
Some of the ladders are very steep!

Climbers can see farms and villages from the top of the rock.

Visitors can climb the steep ladders to the top of Bukit Kelam.

Torres del Paine

Location: Torres del Paine National Park, Chile

The Torres del Paine, or Towers of Paine, are three enormous rocks. Each of the towers is over 2000 metres high.

The Towers of Paine are part of the Torres del Paine National Park in Chile, a country in South America.

Over millions of years, glaciers eroded the rocks into the shapes they are today.

The Towers of Paine are very difficult and dangerous to climb. However, experienced climbers enjoy the challenge.

The national park around these monoliths are home to many wild animals, such as pumas.

a puma

Paine means "blue" in the language of one of the First Nations peoples of South America. *Torres* is the Spanish word for "towers". "Torres del Paine" means "blue towers".

Scullin and Murray Monoliths

Location: Antarctica

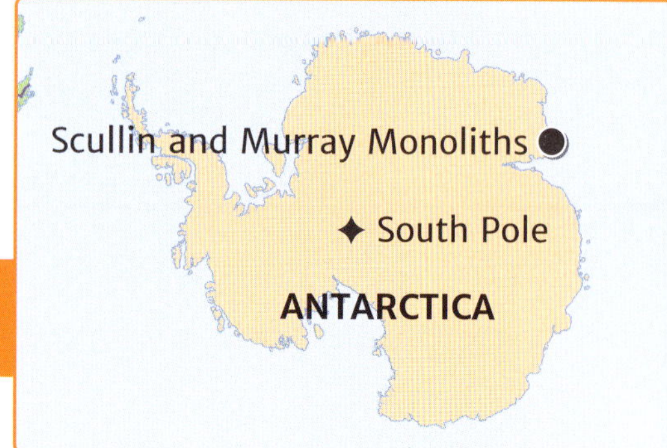

The Scullin and Murray Monoliths are two monoliths off the icy coast of Antarctica. These two cold mountains of rock are just a few kilometres apart. They are surrounded by the sea, which is frozen in winter.

The monoliths were first visited by explorers in the 1930s.

Scullin Monolith

Murray Monolith

Scullin and Murray Monoliths are home to many seabirds. The seabirds raise their chicks on the monoliths. Seals also live on and around them.

Tourists do not visit these monoliths. Scientists sometimes visit them, to study the animals and plants that live there.

Southern giant petrels nest on Scullin and Murray Monoliths.

Around 70 000 pairs of Adelie penguins live on Scullin and Murray Monoliths.

Monoliths are beautiful and important landforms.
These amazing giants of stone help show us how Earth is changed and shaped over time by erosion.
Monoliths provide homes to endangered plants and animals.
Brave climbers enjoy exploring their rocky heights and visitors travel from all over the world to see them.

A tourist takes a photo of Stawamus Chief monolith in British Columbia, Canada.

My Visit to Uluru

Dear Mum and Dad,
I am enjoying my holiday in Central Australia with Grandma and Grandpa.

Yesterday we flew to an airport near Uluru. Uluru is an *amazing* monolith in the desert. Monoliths are enormous rocks or stones. I could see Uluru from the plane window.

Grandma told me that the Anangu people are the traditional owners of Uluru.

We stayed overnight at a hotel.

This morning we got up very early to see the sunrise at Uluru. We caught a bus that took us to the best place to see it.

We took lots of photos as the sun turned the rock shades of gold and red.

After sunrise, clouds came across the sky.
Then it began to rain hard.

I was disappointed by the rain, because we were doing a walking tour around the base of Uluru with a traditional owner.
But he told us not to worry.
He said we might see something special.

We went back to our bus and watched Uluru.
More rain fell, and then lots of waterfalls began to run down the sides of the rock.
It was such a beautiful sight.

I'm glad we visited Uluru when it rained.
Visiting Uluru has been the best part of our holiday!

Love from,
Maddie

Glossary

Antarctica (*proper noun*)
the huge area of land around the South Pole

erosion (*noun*) the wearing away or breaking down of land

First Nations peoples (*proper noun*)
the first peoples living in an area or country

glaciers (*noun*) rivers of solid ice that move very slowly

nature reserve (*noun*) a piece of land that is a protected area for plants and animals

peaks (*noun*) the highest points of monoliths or mountain ranges

sacred (*adjective*) important and highly respected within religious beliefs

territory (*noun*) an area of land that is controlled by a country

traditional owners (*noun*)
the people who have lived on and cared for the land for a long time

Index